SandCastle

Word Families Set 4

-ug as in bug

Nancy Tuminelly

Consulting Editor Monica Marx, M.A./Reading Specialist

ABDO Publishing Company

Published by SandCastle™, an imprint of ABDO Publishing Company, 4940 Viking Drive,
Edina, Minnesota 55435.

Printed in the United States.

Credits
Edited by: Pam Price
Curriculum Coordinator: Nancy Tuminelly
Cover and Interior Design and Production: Mighty Media
Photo Credits: Brand X Pictures, Comstock, Corbis Images, Corel, Kelly Doudna, Hemera,
Image Source Limited, PhotoDisc, Stockbyte

Library of Congress Cataloging-in-Publication Data

Tuminelly, Nancy, 1952-
    -Ug as in bug / Nancy Tuminelly.
        p. cm. -- (Word families. Set IV)
    Summary: Introduces, in brief text and illustrations, the use of the letter combination
"ug" in such words as "bug," "shrug," "drug," and "lug."
    ISBN 1-59197-243-4
    1. Readers (Primary) [1. Vocabulary. 2. Reading.] I. Title.

PE1119 .T836 2003
428.1--dc21
                                                        2002038637

SandCastle™ books are created by a professional team of educators, reading specialists, and
content developers around five essential components that include phonemic awareness,
phonics, vocabulary, text comprehension, and fluency. All books are written, reviewed, and
leveled for guided reading, early intervention reading, and Accelerated Reader® programs
and designed for use in shared, guided, and independent reading and writing activities to
support a balanced approach to literacy instruction.

Let Us Know

After reading the book, SandCastle would like you to tell us your
stories about reading. What is your favorite page? Was there something
hard that you needed help with? Share the ups and downs of learning
to read. We want to hear from you! To get posted on the ABDO
Publishing Company Web site, send us e-mail at:

sandcastle@abdopub.com

SandCastle Level: Transitional

-ug Words

bug

jug

mug

pug

rug

slug

Cindy has a bug in
a jar.

Dad pours milk from
a jug.

Chris is holding a mug.

A pug is a type of dog.

Sara and Mac are
reading on the rug.

The slug is on a log.

Tug the Bug

Tug the bug
was feeling smug.

10

He said, "Bet I can jump
over that jug!"

Tug the bug
jumped over the jug

12

and landed in a mug!

Tug the bug
jumped out of the mug

and landed on a rug
by a slug!

Tug the bug
said goodbye
to the slug.

He jumped off of the rug

and onto a plug.

Tug the bug
hopped off the plug

and landed on
Dug the pug.

Dug the pug
gave a shrug,

then Tug gave Dug
a snug hug!

The -ug Word Family

bug	plug
drug	pug
Dug	rug
glug	shrug
hug	slug
jug	smug
lug	snug
mug	Tug

Glossary

Some of the words in this list may have more than one meaning. The meaning listed here reflects the way the word is used in the book.

bug   an insect

jug   a large container with a small opening and a handle

pug   a dog with a flat nose, short hair, and a wrinkled face

slug   a slimy creature that looks like a snail without a shell

About SandCastle™

A professional team of educators, reading specialists, and content developers created the SandCastle™ series to support young readers as they develop reading skills and strategies and increase their general knowledge. The SandCastle™ series has four levels that correspond to early literacy development in young children. The levels are provided to help teachers and parents select the appropriate books for young readers.

Emerging Readers
(no flags)

Beginning Readers
(1 flag)

Transitional Readers
(2 flags)

Fluent Readers
(3 flags)

These levels are meant only as a guide. All levels are subject to change.

To see a complete list of SandCastle™ books and other nonfiction titles from ABDO Publishing Company, visit www.abdopub.com or contact us at:

4940 Viking Drive, Edina, Minnesota 55435 • 1-800-800-1312 • fax: 1-952-831-1632